HENRY's STARS

David Elliot

Philomel Books

An Imprint of Penguin Group (USA)

Henry sat quietly on his step, staring up at the night sky.

It was a beautiful warm evening, and as he looked from star to star, they seemed to form a picture in the darkness.

"Oh!" he squealed. "What's that?"

"It's a great big starry pig
running across the sky!"

Henry raced over to the woolshed,
where Maisie, Daisy, and Clementine were
getting ready for bed.

"Baaa! What's all the excitement,
Henry?" they bleated.

"I've found the Great Pig in the Sky,"
squealed Henry.

"Where? Show us!" said the sheep.

"There are his ears, and there are his legs,
and there is his curly tail," he said, pointing
at a group of stars. "See?"

Maisie, Daisy, and Clementine
looked where Henry pointed.

"Ah, yes! I see it!" said Daisy. "There is a sheep's ear and woolly body. How clever you are, Henry—you have found a Great Sheep."

Just then, Abigail came sauntering over.
"What are you doing?" she asked. "Shouldn't
you all be in bed?"

"Baaa! We've found the Great Sheep of the Stars,"
cried Maisie, Daisy, and Clementine triumphantly.

"Great Pig, actually," said Henry.

Abigail looked at the stars.
She craned her head and whisked
her tail.
"Ah, yes! I see it!" she mooed
excitedly.

"There is a cow's horn," said Abigail,
waving her hoof at the sky, "and a handsome
cow's tail. It's definitely a Great Star Cow,
and she looks hungry. She thinks she may
just eat those stars over there!"

Just then, Mr. Brown came plodding over the yard. "What's all this?" he whinnied. "Why are you all staring into the sky?"

"We've found the Great Star Cow," mooed Abigail.

"The Great Sheep of the Stars, actually,"
said Maisie, Daisy, and Clementine,
frowning.

Henry just sighed.

"Move over. I'll settle this," said Mr. Brown,
getting himself comfortable.
They all waited while Mr. Brown looked
carefully at the sky.

"Ah, yes! I see it!" he snorted finally. "It's a Great Starry Horse. I see his head and his mane and his hooves flying. He's galloping like the wind. How nice of you to find him."

"You mean the Great Star Cow," said Abigail indignantly.

"Baaa! He means the Great Sheep of the Stars," argued the sheep.

By now, the chickens
had joined in.

"Look," they squawked, pointing their wings. "Heavenly Hens flying all over the place!"

"EXCUSE ME!" said Henry sternly. "There are no Great Sheep of the Stars or Great Star Cows or Great Starry Horses or Heavenly Hens. There is just my Great Pig, and that's that!"

But now, when he looked up at where the Great Pig once was, all he saw was a sheep's ear next to a cow's horn on a galloping horse's body.

What happened to his Great Pig? he wondered.

Henry sighed, his mind all aclutter.
He decided to go back home.

He sat forlornly on his step and stared up
at the sky. He was beginning to think that
his friends might be right. Maybe there was
no Great Pig after all.

But as he sat there wondering, slowly the squabbles of the farmyard dwindled away into the night, and Henry found himself alone again with his stars.

"Oh!" he squealed. "I see it! I see it!"

There, running in starlight across the night
once more, was Henry's Great Pig.

Henry couldn't wait to show the others.

For Semadar

ALSO BY DAVID ELLIOT

Henry's Map

PHILOMEL BOOKS
Published by the Penguin Group
Penguin Group (USA) LLC
375 Hudson Street, New York, NY 10014

USA | Canada | UK | Ireland | Australia | New Zealand | India | South Africa | China
penguin.com
A Penguin Random House Company

Library of Congress Cataloging-in-Publication Data
Elliot, David, 1952– author, illustrator.
Henry's stars / David Elliot.   pages cm   Summary: Henry the pig is excited to spot the Great Pig in the Sky one starry night, but when he shows the other farm animals, he gets frustrated because they each see something different.   [1. Constellations—Fiction. 2. Pigs—Fiction. 3. Domestic animals—Fiction. 4. Farm life—Fiction.] I. Title.   PZ7.E4315Hes 2015
[E]—dc23   2014033929
Manufactured in China by South China Printing Co. Ltd.
ISBN 978-0-399-17116-1
1 3 5 7 9 10 8 6 4 2

Edited by Michael Green. | Design by Semadar Megged. | Text set in 17-point Neutraface Text.
The illustrations were created with pencil and watercolor, and some technology.